#12 Gecko Gladiator

Books in the
S.W.I.T.C.H. series

#12 Gecko Gladiator

Ali Sparkes

illustrated by
Ross Collins

MINNEAPOLIS

Darby Creek
A division of Lerner Publishing Group, Inc.
241 First Avenue North
Minneapolis, MN 55401 U.S.A.

For reading levels and more invormation, look up this title at
www.lernerbooks.com

Main body text set in ITC Goudy Sans Std. 14/19.
Typeface provided by Monotype Typography.

Library of Congress Cataloging-in-Publication Data
Sparkes, Ali.
    Gecko gladiator / by Ali Sparkes ; illustrated by Ross Collins.
        pages   cm. — (S.W.I.T.C.H. ; #12)
    "Originally published by Oxford University Press in 2011."
    Summary: Twins Danny and Josh reveal to neighbor Petty Potts that they
have been on a quest to find marbles containing secret code and soon find
themselves—as geckos—in her new secret laboratory within the very pink
Princessland.
    ISBN 978-1-4677-2115-8 (lib. bdg. : alk. paper)
    ISBN 978-1-4677-2418-0 (eBook)
    [1. Ciphers—Fiction. 2. Geckos—Fiction. 3. Brothers—Fiction.
4. Twins—Fiction. 5. Science fiction.] I. Collins, Ross, illustrator. II. Title.
PZ7.S73712Gec 2014
[Fic]—dc23   2013019715

Manufactured in the United States of America
1 – SB – 12/31/13

To Jacob James Harley Stewart
(who keeps his socks on to read in bed)

With grateful thanks to
John Buckley and Tony Gent of
Amphibian and Reptile Conservation
for their hot-blooded guidance on
S.W.I.T.C.H.'s cold-blooded reptile heroes

Danny and Josh and Petty

Josh and Danny might be twins, but they're NOT the same. Josh loves getting his hands dirty and learning about nature. Danny thinks Josh is a nerd. Skateboarding and climbing are way cooler! And their next-door neighbor, Petty, is only interested in one thing . . . her top secret S.W.I.T.C.H. potion.

Danny

- FULL NAME: Danny Phillips
- AGE: eight years
- HEIGHT: taller than Josh
- FAVORITE THING: skateboarding
- WORST THING: creepy-crawlies and cleaning
- AMBITION: to be a stuntman

Josh

- FULL NAME: Josh Phillips
- AGE: eight years
- HEIGHT: taller than Danny
- FAVORITE THING: collecting insects
- WORST THING: skateboarding
- AMBITION: to be an entomologist

Petty

- FULL NAME: Petty Hortense Potts
- AGE: none of your business
- HEIGHT: head and shoulders above every other scientist
- FAVORITE THING: S.W.I.T.C.H.ing Josh & Danny
- WORST THING: evil ex-friend Victor Crouch
- AMBITION: adoration and recognition as the world's most genius scientist (and for the government to say sorry!)

Contents

A Poxy Situation

"Do you think she's dead?"

Danny, wobbling on Josh's shoulders, peered through the dusty window into Petty Potts's front room. He didn't answer his twin brother but pressed his nose up hard against the glass, trying to see past the grimy net curtains and figure out whether the large blue shape on the sofa was moving.

"Danny!" hissed Josh. "You're breaking my back!" He was doubled up, supporting his brother's weight. His forehead was grinding against the damp red brick under their neighbor's windowsill. "Is she dead?!"

"It's hard to say," muttered Danny. "I mean— she never looks all that healthy at the best of times, does she?"

"No—but she doesn't usually look like a corpse!" grunted Josh. "Is she moving?"

Danny got up onto his feet, treading carefully on each of his brother's shoulder blades, hanging on to Petty's rather rotten window frame. The top panes didn't have nets, so they'd be easier to see through.

"I can't hold you up any longer!" gurgled Josh, but he didn't have to. Three seconds later, there was a creak and a crack and a crash. Danny had fallen through the window.

"Gah!" remarked Josh, in surprise. He stood up and glanced all around,

guiltily. Had anybody seen his brother accidentally breaking and entering? No . . . there was nobody around. "Danny! Are you OK!" he whispered. He peered inside through the broken glass and wood. Below he could make out Danny, struggling out of a dusty, gray net curtain, spluttering.

"OK—I'm coming in!" Josh said, carefully climbing through. It was a good thing, really, that the wooden frame had been weak. Even if it meant that Petty's window had been smashed. If they'd broken down her front door, they would probably be skewered on the ends of poison-dipped spears by now. Or reduced to a heap of ash and charred bones or something. Petty had put some formidable defenses in place in her house recently. But amazingly, she had failed to secure the window.

Danny had escaped the dusty net curtain by the time Josh jumped down next to him—and he wasn't cut by broken glass. That was good news. On the other hand, Petty was still motionless on the sofa. That was not so good. They looked at each other, gulping.

From this angle, they could only see her gray mop of hair. It was hard to tell whether she was dead or alive. As he got closer, Danny could see one small patch of wrinkled cheek. He prodded it gingerly with one finger. "It's warm!" he said, with relief. And then he shrieked as Petty's hand suddenly swiped up and grabbed his wrist.

There was a moment of silence during which Petty eased herself up on one elbow and peered at him. "Hello, Danny," she croaked. "Hello, Josh. What, exactly, are you doing in my front parlor?"

"We came to find out if you were still alive," Danny said, panting with relief. "You haven't been answering the door for days, and we thought you might have died."

"Oh really?" Petty raised an eyebrow behind her smeary spectacles.

"Well, you know . . . you are quite old," Danny said.

"Danny!" Josh kicked his brother's ankle. "Don't be rude!"

"No—not a bit of it!" Petty said, sitting up properly now. "After all, I am ancient. It's a wonder

I can even walk, talk, or safely visit the toilet. My heart could pop. I could just keel over at any time. Just one loud noise or a funny smell, and it could be curtains for Old Granny Potts. Better not stand too close to me when you've got an attack of flatulence, Danny. You could take us both out."

"So—why didn't you answer our calls? Our knocks? Our doorbell ringing?" asked Josh.

"I have had chicken pox," Petty said. And now that they looked closely, they could see that she had a rash of rather nasty red pimples—many of them topped with a little yellow crust. "I've been dreadfully tired and sore. And I didn't feel like talking to anyone—or infecting anyone!"

Josh and Danny took a step back.

"Oh don't fret now!" Petty said. "I'm not infectious anymore. Once the spots get all scabby, you're past the point of infecting anyone."

"Phew," sighed Danny, sinking into a worn leather armchair. "We thought it was all over for the S.W.I.T.C.H. Project."

"I'm touched by your concern," Petty said. "But now that you're here, I might as well get out the chocolate cake. And then you can tell me about . . . this!" She dug in her pocket and held out something small, round, and shiny.

"Our marble!" breathed Josh. "Yes—and—well, you might want to look at these too." He dug in his own pocket and withdrew a small black drawstring bag. In it were two marbles. One blue and one red. "These two are like the green one you've got there. They have a code in them and a hologram—just like your BUGSWITCH and REPTOSWITCH cubes."

Petty stared at the marbles in Josh's palm as if she was desperately trying to remember something. After thirty seconds, she got unsteadily to her feet. "No—no good!" she snapped. "Until I have chocolate cake and a large mug of tea, not a single synapse is going to fire!"

"She means her brain isn't working," muttered Josh to Danny, following Petty into the kitchen. "Sit down, Petty. We'll get it," he said, feeling guilty because she really did look pretty bad. She was pale under the pox. He and Danny put the kettle on and got the cake out of a tin in the fridge. Petty sat at the table rolling the three coded marbles around in her hand.

Soon they were all munching cake covered with thick chocolate icing and gulping down hot brown tea between bites. Petty's color began to improve. The glimmer returned to her eyes as she continued to stare closely at the marbles.

"So," she said, eventually. "Where did these come from?"

Josh and Danny looked at each other and then back at Petty. "We were hoping you could tell us," Josh said. "They've been sent to *us*—by the Mystery Marble Sender. One at a time across the last three weeks or so. We thought maybe it was you."

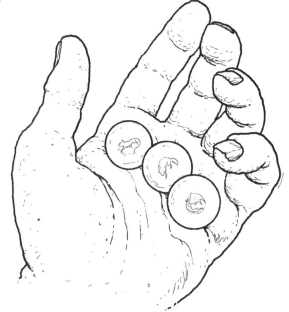

"Why on earth would it be *me?*" Petty asked.

"Well . . . because they've got a code in them. And a hologram," explained Josh. "Just like in your S.W.I.T.C.H. cubes! We didn't think anybody else could make Serum Which Instigates Total Cellular Hijack."

"And nobody else can!" agreed Petty. "I made these, yes—I told you! But I can't remember when. Or why. Or what for. Remember that nasty bag of bones Victor Crouch burnt out my memory after he tried to steal my S.W.I.T.C.H. Project work and claim it as his own! There are big echoing chambers of my brain with VACANT signs hung over them, thanks to my backstabbing former best friend."

"Well . . . maybe Victor Crouch *did* manage to steal some of your formula after all—this bit," Danny said.

"It looks like a S.W.I.T.C.H. code for mammals," Josh said. "We had a look with my microscope. There's a bat shape in the blue one and a cat shape in the red one."

"There's a wolf shape in the green one," Petty said. "I started on insects with BUGSWITCH. Then rediscovered amphibians and reptiles after you helped me find the missing cubes containing the code to REPTOSWITCH. If I had been working in any kind of order, the next thing I would have created would certainly have been MAMMALSWITCH." She smiled. "I really am fabulously good! Top-caliber genius!"

"But who sent these to us?" insisted Josh. "If it wasn't you."

"Well, why would it be me, you twaddlehead?" Petty said. "Why would I exclude you from a brand-new, exciting S.W.I.T.C.H. phase? And then send you vital parts of it anonymously? You and Danny are my assistants. I need your help. And when the S.W.I.T.C.H. formulas are all finally perfected, you will join me on the world's stage as the assistants of the GREATEST GENIUS SCIENTIST IN THE HISTORY OF MANKIND!!!" This last she said as an echoing shout, rising to her feet and raising her chocolatey hands as if she were already on a stage being cheered by thousands of other, less clever scientists.

"She's so modest," muttered Danny.

"Hmmm . . ." Petty sank back down onto her kitchen chair and cut herself a second slice of cake. "Did this Mystery Marble Sender include a note with the other marbles?"

"Yes—a note always comes first," Josh said. "With a clue to find the next marble." He put several bits of paper with spiky handwriting on them into Petty's hand. "So far we've found one marble in a barn owl's nest, one up in a light in the school hall, and one—last week—in a ruined sea fort."

"Whoever it is," Danny said, "they're spying on us and following us around. They even followed us on holiday!"

"Or they were following *me*," Petty said, scanning the notes. "Remember I was at your holiday beach too. Far more likely, it's all about me . . ."

"Even though they were all addressed to us?" snorted Josh.

"That's just to throw me off the scent," murmured Petty. "It's all about me."

"So modest," muttered Danny.

"I'm going to have to pack up my lab and go even sooner than I thought," Petty said, slapping the notes down on the table. "First, the attempted break-in—now notes to you which are clearly meant for ME! It's getting more dangerous here by the minute!"

"But—where will you go?" asked Josh, appalled. "And . . . what about the rest of the

REPTOSWITCH project. You were going to S.W.I.T.C.H. us into snakes and—and—"

"Alligators!" continued Danny, forlornly biting into his second slice of cake. "Fwee fwant koo be falligators!"

"Don't talk with your mouth full," chided Petty. "And don't be so selfish! Can't you see? They're closing in! If my lab gets discovered, I'll be kidnapped and tortured for all my secrets! And so, very possibly, will you! I don't think it's safe for you to come around here and see me anymore."

"What?" Danny stood up. "After all we've done for you! You're just going to chuck us off the S.W.I.T.C.H. Project?"

"Don't be so melodramatic, Danny!" Petty stood up too. "I mean, I think you'll have to meet me somewhere else . . . in my new secret lab!"

"Your new lab? Is it ready?" Josh asked.

"Very nearly," Petty said. "In fact . . . I will let you see it tomorrow. Take this." She dug into her other pocket and then handed Josh a small, white spray bottle with a big *G* written on it in marker. "It will allow you to find your way in. Do NOT

use it before you reach the new address. Josh—
I'm trusting you not to let Danny persuade you
before then."

"Hey!" Danny said, looking wounded.

"Only when you get there!" went on Petty. "Or
I won't trust you again. And make sure you're not
followed."

Josh grabbed the S.W.I.T.C.H. spray bottle.
A surge of deep excitement ran through him.
"Which S.W.I.T.C.H. is it?" he breathed.

"You'll find out soon enough," Petty said. "Meet me here . . ."—she handed Danny a scrap of paper with an address written on it—". . . at 2 p.m. tomorrow."

"Here?" Danny said, puzzled.

"All will become clear," Petty said, making what she obviously thought was a mysterious expression but looking really more as if she had a bad case of gas. "Now—off you go. Unless you want to help me apply baking soda to my pustules . . ."

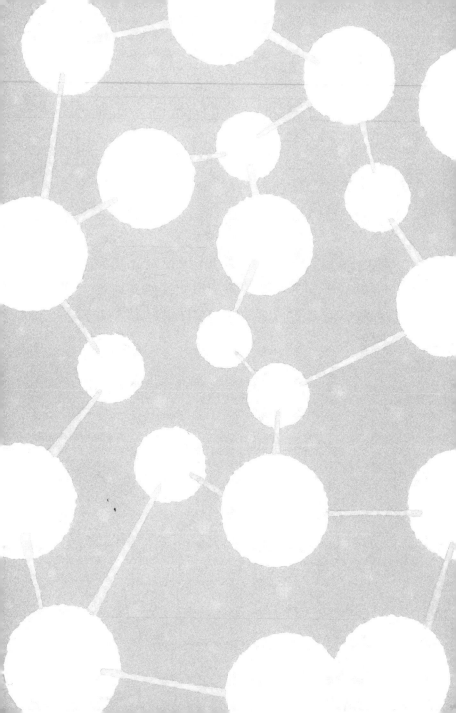

Princessland

"Oh no," Danny said. "Oh no, oh no, oh no!"

"Errm," added Josh.

This was worse than they had imagined. Far worse.

The brothers stood, frozen, in front of a large warehouse-style shop. It was located in a strip mall about twenty minutes' walk from their house. Mom and Dad thought they'd gone up to the park. They would be amazed if they saw where their sons really were at this moment. Standing outside PRINCESSLAND.

"This has got to be a mistake!" Danny peered at the address on the note again. But no—the number above the door of Princessland was unmistakably 18. Danny had been surprised enough when Petty had written down Unit 18,

RAINBOW BUSINESS PARK—but this? "This can't be right," he went on. "She's a genius scientist! She should be building her lab in a hollowed-out extinct volcano!"

"Not many of those around here," pointed out Josh.

"All right then—an old water tower. An abandoned nuclear waste dump—I don't know. Anything but this!" Danny's voice wobbled as he stared up again at Princessland. It was a shop filled with lovely things for lovely girls. Dresses and shoes and tiaras and tie-on fairy wings and dollies and little shiny handbags and strawberry-flavored lip gloss and . . .

"Face it," Josh said. "Petty Potts has gone to Princessland." It sounded a bit like a kind way of saying someone had died or gone mad . . . and as far as Danny was concerned, it was the same.

"I'm not walking in there!" he said. "Let's use the S.W.I.T.C.H. spray and go inside in disguise."

"No," Josh said. "For one thing, we don't know what we're going to turn into, do we? *G* could stand for anything in the reptile world . . . It could be a Gila Monster. Half a meter long with a venomous bite. Or a Galápagos tortoise—way too slow to get away before the Humane Society shows up. And for another thing—read that!"

There was a note at the bottom of the address. It read: "Go to the lobby at the back and S.W.I.T.C.H. to get in under the red door. BEWARE! NOBODY MUST SEE! Keep a low profile."

"Keep a low profile?" spluttered Danny. "In Princessland, when we're *boys*? Is she nuts?"

Josh shrugged. There was no need to answer that one. He grabbed Danny's arm. "Come on. If we stand out here much longer, we'll attract attention. Just walk in. We can pretend we're buying a birthday present for our sister."

"Jenny's fourteen. I think she's grown out of fairy wings!" Danny hissed.

"We can pretend she's four," Josh said.

Inside Princessland, it was every bit as bad as Danny had feared. As soon as they stepped through the door, three sparkly fairies on springs bounced down into their faces, saying things like, "Hi there, best friend!" and "The fairies love YOU!" and "Let's go shopping in the Fairyland mall!" Danny screamed and swatted them away as if he was being attacked by wasps. Wasps styled by Disney.

Danny ducked away and nearly knocked into a big whiteboard with PARTY TIME! written on it in glittery purple pen. "Princessland welcomes Princess Megan and all her friends to a Damsels' Party at 4 p.m. today!"

"I mean—what does that even *mean*?" he found himself wondering. "Does anyone really know what a damsel is?"

"It's a kind of princess, I think," Josh said. "Usually in distress. And they seem to wear cone-y things with ribbons on their heads . . ."

"You know too much," muttered Danny, darkly.

He shuddered and turned to look at the large shop floor. It was festooned in glittering pink, yellow, and purple displays of girly stuff. There were huge TV screens dangling from the ceiling all around the store. Endless commercials with nonstop tinkly music advertised all the girly toys available. Even the *Darcy Show* was getting in on the act. Mom and Jenny's favorite talk-show host, wearing her trademark yellow jacket and black sequinned pants, was gushing about her own tiny doll—the Diddly DeeDee—and her own brand of toy microphone. A rack of sparkly yellow My Little Microphones stood to their left, just behind the attack fairies. Danny and Josh stared past it, trying to work out the quickest route to the red door that Petty had mentioned. It was clear they would have to cross all the way to the back of the store.

"Do we really have to do this?" Danny wailed.

Josh grabbed his arm again. "Stop freaking out!" he snapped. "Remember! Low profile!"

But Danny's fight with the fairies had already attracted attention. At least six girls were now peering at them, giggling in pairs. One small girl and her mother just glanced at them with disdain and then hurried around a corner. Josh dragged Danny along the Diddly DeeDee aisle. Its tall shelves were packed with tiny, pink dolls and a phenomenal amount of clothes and accessories, most of which could fit into a matchbox. "Why do they have to be so yellow and purple and pink?" Danny murmured. "Why are girls so nuts about pink? PINK!"

"Just don't look," Josh advised his brother, as Danny's eyes started to get fixed. "Now—you see the My Tiny Horsey rotating display? We've got to get to the far side of that . . ."

"My Tiny Horsey?" whimpered Danny, his eyes going glassy. He'd seen the commercials for My Tiny Horsey on TV. My Tiny Horsey had eyelashes and necklaces and manes and tails of different colors. And you could put special glittery nail polish on its hooves . . .

"Snap out of it!" hissed Josh, whacking Danny on the back of the head. "It's just girls' toys! Pretend they're all called DEATHKILL STALLION and they're black and gray and carrying machine guns and you'll be OK!"

Danny did his best. Despite some giggling very close behind him and a definite whiff of glittery hoof polish, he got to the far side of the display alongside Josh. Here they nearly collided with the mother and daughter who had scurried away from them earlier. Both wore identical long, lumpy, dark coats, even though it was quite warm outside. And both of them had identical curly brown hair and gray eyes, which they narrowed suspiciously at Josh and Danny. The girl was not much older than Josh and Danny. But she looked as disapprovingly as her mother as they stalked away, wrapping their coats tightly around them.

"I thought they were going to start hissing at us for a moment there," Danny said. "What's their problem?"

"Never mind," breathed Josh, tugging Danny across to the lobby area. "We've made it."

"Aaaargh!" shrieked Danny. Accidentally, he had snagged a pair of pink and gold fairy wings on his shoulder as he'd run through the dress-up aisle. "GETITOFFMEEE!" he wailed. And Josh, with a weary sigh, removed the wings as if they were a large moth. He ducked back into the aisle and hung them up on the fairy dress-up display. "Take home a Diddly DeeDee today," urged the *Darcy Show* presenter from a nearby screen. "She's just like me . . . only Diddly Deeee!"

Josh ran away.

"Come on—look—there's the red door," he said, as soon as he got back. And there it was, tucked out of sight around the corner from the shop floor. Next to it was a blue door with a PRIVATE sign on it. On the red door, there was just one small paper sign taped into place. It read MUTATIO INC.

"Mutatio?" Danny whispered. "What's that got to do with Petty Potts?"

"It's Latin," Josh said. "I think it means 'change' or . . . 'switch.'" Josh had picked up quite a bit of Latin because of all the Latin names of wildlife he'd read about.

He tried the door. It was locked. Of course, he'd known it would be. Why would they need to S.W.I.T.C.H. if they could just walk in? He got out the spray bottle and glanced around. Nobody was anywhere near them. They were tucked out of sight of the main store. Despite all the fuss Danny had made, there was no sign of any member of the staff coming. "Come on," he said. "Let's S.W.I.T.C.H."

He sprayed them both. A few seconds later, the red door shot up to the size of a house as he and Danny shrank down to their new shape and size. The crack under the door now looked like the gap you'd find beneath a bench. Easy to get under.

"Oh-ho-hoho!" marveled Danny, staring at his brother. "That is really cool!"

There was a metal kick plate at the bottom of the red door. Josh looked at his reflection to see what he had become. "Wow! I'm a gecko!" Josh breathed. He checked the underside of his feet. "A tokay gecko! WOW!"

He was a magnificent sight. A neat, sleek lizard covered in fabulous fine yellow scales with orange and blue spots. His belly was a pale milk white, and his face was lit up by two dark, glinting, orblike eyes. His snout was rounded, with a wide, smiling mouth. His feet were dainty. Their five toes had squishy pads on them, which made them look like the petals on a flower. Josh knew

these "petals" were one of the most amazing
things about his new form—he couldn't wait to
find out if they really worked. Turning, he checked
out his tail. It was long and leaf-shaped, tapering
to a neat point.

"Oh great," Danny said, also staring into the
metal mirror. "Oh—just great!"

Danny was much like Josh in shape and size,
from his big eyes and petal-shaped toes to his tail.

But there were two differences.

He was stripy.

And he was pink.

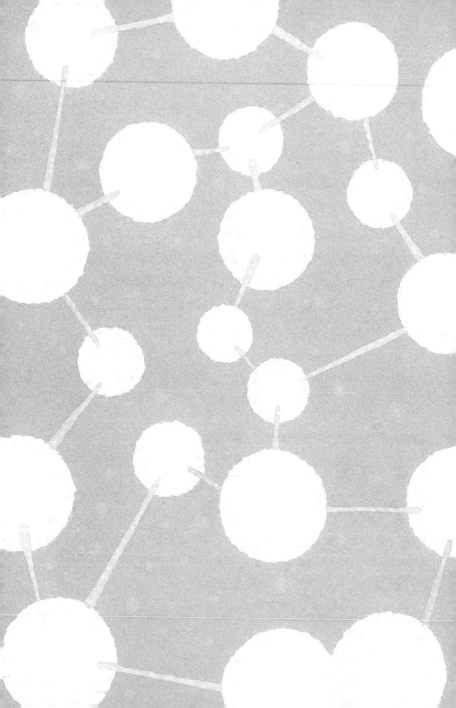

Pretty in Pink

Josh laughed so hard he thought his inner gecko workings might burst. "But, Danny . . ." he spluttered, between a series of high-pitched chirrups and clicks, "you're so pretty!"

Danny smacked Josh in the face with his tail and scurried under the door. On the other side, there was a cliff of concrete. Followed by another cliff of concrete. And then another. A staircase.

Josh arrived at his side, still shaking with laughter. He opened his mouth to say something, but Danny gave him a fierce stare. "DON'T!" was all he said, and Josh bit down on his next joke. After all Danny's freaking out about the pink and glittery stuff in the shop, he could have been designed by Princessland.

Of course, Josh was a very pretty gecko too—but the orange and blue spots weren't at all girly. Why they'd both S.W.I.T.C.H.ed with such different colors, Josh couldn't say. Maybe it was just Danny's inner pinkness coming out.

"So," Danny said, pinkly. "What's going to eat us today?"

"We're not in much danger here," grinned Josh. "Unless Petty's bought herself a cat. Come on—I've got something to show you!" And Josh ran up the step. Literally—up it. He didn't even have to try to work out how to reach the first ledge and haul himself up. He ran up the smooth concrete without any difficulty at all.

"Whoa! Let me try!" Danny said, following his brother. He'd been climbing as a lizard before. But that had been up a tree with lots of easy claw-holds to help. This surface was completely flat and smooth. As a sand lizard, he would have struggled—but as a gecko . . . no problem!

Ahead of him, Josh wasn't bothering with the stairs at all—he was just scampering up the wall of the stairwell, heading for the ceiling in a straight line. He was letting out little squeaks and clicks of excitement that echoed off the hard, plastered walls. "You see these?" He lifted one foot and showed off its toes. Underneath each toe was a group of tiny white mushroom-like things. "They're called setae!" chirruped Josh. "They stick like glue every time we press them against the wall— they're incredibly strong! But then they just pop off again when we want to carry on. Scientists all over the world have been trying to make something that does what a gecko's foot does! I was reading about it just last week!"

Danny caught up with his brother. He'd forgotten his unfortunate color now and was hugely enjoying the climb. "We're like Spider-Man!" he marveled.

"Yeah—except that Spider-Man is pretend—and geckos do it for real!" Josh grinned at his brother in delight, revealing a row of small, sharp teeth. "Now watch this!" And he ran right up to the top of the wall and effortlessly flipped his lizardy body upside down before walking jauntily across the ceiling. "Whoooo-hooo! Look at meeee!" he called.

Danny wasted no time in following him. Walking upside down on the ceiling was amazing . . . although he and Josh had done it once before. "We did this when we were flies, remember?" he said.

"Yeah . . . and that was cool too," Josh said. "But now we're doing it with style. We're not just about to go and vomit all over someone's cake mix, are we? This time, we're beautiful!"

"And we can't get eaten by a spider," added Danny, happily.

"Nope . . . we eat the spider!" Josh said. "Fancy a snack?" And he ran toward the corner of the stairwell ceiling where a few spindly cellar spiders hung in fine strands of web. As soon as they saw him, they began to swing around wildly.

They hoped to put him off them by seeming bigger than they were through the wild, blurry movements. Josh was very tempted to snap one up—his lizard instinct was telling him to have some munchies right here, right now.

But he was soft-hearted. He remembered how it felt to be a spider about to be eaten. He couldn't do it. "Come on, Danny," he said, turning away from the arachnid snack counter. "Let's go find Petty."

"OK," Danny said. Three legs were poking out of his mouth.

"You didn't!"

"Didn't what?" asked Danny, innocently, with a gulp.

"Never mind," chuckled Josh. He knew Danny would have blocked out all memory of his little snack already. Josh ran back to the wall and down to another door. At the foot of the door, a greenish shaft of light shone through. He headed for it and slipped easily under the crack. Danny arrived beside him a few seconds later.

They were in a large room under sloping eaves. The loft area, Danny guessed. It was huge at the moment, of course, because they were small lizards. But even as humans, it would be pretty big. Three high windows ran along one side. The slanting windows in the ceiling above would normally let in plenty of light. But they were covered in dark blinds. The room was

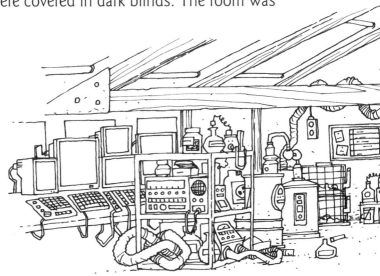

bathed in the green glow of Petty's computer monitors sitting on a high bench. Josh and Danny wandered across the wooden floor, staring all around them. The room was clearly a laboratory. One much bigger than the laboratory beneath Petty's garden shed. Its many shelves and tables were filled with bottles and boxes and Bunsen burners and test tubes and weird gadgets of every kind. A large mouse cage took up one corner. And in the center was a familiar square tent of plastic—the S.W.I.T.C.H.ing chamber.

"Well," Petty said, stepping out of the chamber and peering down at them in the dim light. "What do you think?"

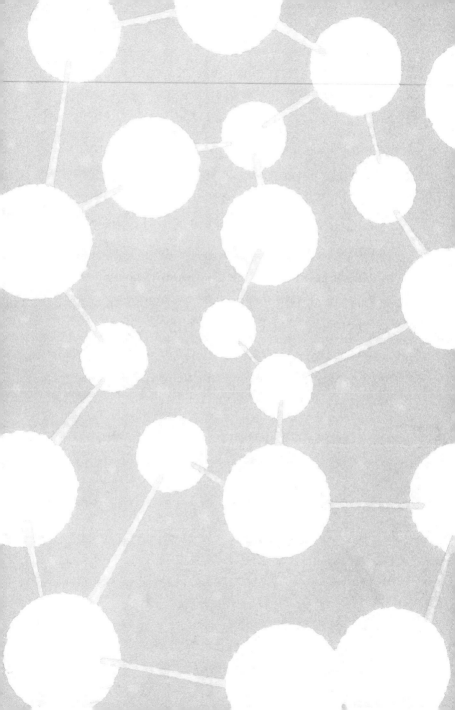

Bang to Wrongs

Josh and Danny tried to tell her how impressed they were—but all that came out were those chirruping, clicking, and occasionally grunting noises.

"Aaah—geckos! The noisiest lizards there are!" Petty said, smiling at them appreciatively. "The only reptiles that can make noises humans can hear, don't you know? Well—one of you *is* a pretty boy!" she added. She knelt down and patted Danny on the head. He growled.

"But I need you to S.W.I.T.C.H. back now so we can talk," Petty said. And she swiftly squirted them with a bottle of antidote spray.

"Aa-aaw!" Josh was disappointed. "I wanted to walk across your ceiling!"

"Plenty of time for that later," Petty said.

"How come he got to be all cool with spots and I turned into Barbie Gecko?" snapped Danny, folding his arms with a huff.

"Well, you're very much the same—it's just a skin pigment issue," Petty said. "Although it does suggest that the formula is a little unstable . . . again." She looked slightly concerned.

"Unstable? That'll be the third unstable S.W.I.T.C.H. you've let us try!" squeaked Danny.

"The second," corrected Petty. "I didn't let you try the TurtleSWITCH, you may recall. You stole it and tried it entirely of your own free will!"

"But the chameleon one was unstable too," argued Danny. "And you let us try that even when your mouse ended up half-rodent, half-chameleon!"

"I don't know why you fuss so," Petty said. "You're always fine in the end. Cutting-edge science can't be perfectly safe. I am a genius, and I must push the boundaries."

"Hmmm," Danny muttered. "Funny how you always push the boundaries from a safe distance! I've never seen *you* try the S.W.I.T.C.H. out!"

"I'm much older than you. My bones are far too brittle," Petty said with a dismissive wave. "Anyway—enough of all this. I wanted you to see my new lab—and here it is!"

"Why have it over Princessland?" Josh asked. "Are you trying to mess with our minds?"

"What did you expect? A hollowed-out, extinct volcano? I am now based here because it is the very last place that government spies would think of looking for me," explained Petty. "And if they see me coming into the store, they'll think I've just come to buy something pretty for a . . . niece or something."

Josh and Danny stared at Petty. They could not imagine her ever buying something from Princessland.

Petty held up a glittery pink bag carrying the store's name. "See!" she said. "I always carry one of these out with me when I go."

"What's in it?" Josh asked.

"Wadded-up tissues, dried calamine lotion, and chicken pox scabs mostly," Petty said, peering into the bag.

There was a short silence and then a further pause while Josh and Danny massaged the rigid masks of horror off their faces.

"Come on, come on—over here!" Petty said. She led them to a corner of the room. There, in a pool of white light from a desk lamp, lay a microscope and several jars and boxes. "I've been studying the marbles. You're right—all three of them contain code for MAMMALSWITCH. I recognize my own brilliant work! I must have made the formula . . . maybe years ago while I was still working for the government. And there are six marbles, the same way there were six BUGSWITCH cubes and six REPTOSWITCH cubes."

"How do you know there are six?" Josh asked.

"Because when I was clearing out the shelves of my old lab, I found this," Petty said. She held up a small box covered in blue velvet. It looked much like the square red and green velvet boxes containing the BUG and REPTILESWITCH cubes—but this box was round. Inside there was a ripple of some silky blue material across six round dents. In three of these, Petty had pressed the first three marbles—red, green, and blue. But the other three dents were empty.

"So . . . did you hide the marbles the same way you hid the REPTOSWITCH cubes?" Danny asked. "In case Victor Crouch double-crossed you and came looking for them?"

"I don't know," sighed Petty. "Obviously that bit of memory is burnt out, or I would have thought to ask you to look for these when I asked you to look for the REPTOSWITCH cubes in the summer. And anyway . . . if I did hide them, somebody else has clearly found them. Or more likely, stolen them."

"Who?" Josh asked. "Victor Crouch again?"

Petty reached behind her and took down a wooden frame. In it, much to their amazement, was a photo of Victor Crouch. He was wearing a black hat and waving cheerily at the photographer, the one spiky black fingernail on his little finger pointing up into the air. Had he possessed any, his eyebrows would have been raised. But as peculiar as Petty's old nemesis looked, it was something else that made them gasp—he had his arm around none other than Petty Potts.

"Yes," sighed Petty. "This was when we were friends . . . or so I thought."

The Petty in the photo looked about ten years younger. Her hair was darker, and she had one or two fewer chins—and those chins were definitely less whiskery. Someone else's hand was tucked through the crook of Petty's left arm, but they were cropped out of the picture.

"This was taken while we were working together in the secret government laboratories," remembered Petty. "Little did I know that only a year or so later, he would have framed me in a very different way! And lost me my job and tried to steal all my genius work! I also found this while clearing out the old lab. I keep it to remind me never to trust anyone! You hear me, boys?" Her voice became shrill as she started bashing the picture against the wall. "Never trust ANYONE! NEVER, NEVER, NEVER!!!" There was a tinkle of broken glass.

"O . . . K," Josh said, stepping away. "So . . . no other ideas about who the Mystery Marble Sender is?"

"Nope," snapped Petty. "Were there postmarks on any of the letters?"

"Only on one parcel," Danny said. "All the others were hand delivered—apart from one which came on a parachute. The parcel had a London postmark. It was a set of books Josh had won in a wildlife competition with Chatz TV. A clue was tucked in with it."

"London . . . hmmm. Well, that's not much help," grunted Petty. She slapped the broken picture frame facedown on her workbench. "No idea at all! And even LESS idea why this Mystery Marble Sender is sending them to YOU two. Go on—go on home now and see if there have been any more clues! Keep watch! Never rest! Watch from behind your curtains at ALL TIMES! If you watch all the time, sooner or later the Mystery Marble Sender will slip up and you'll SEE him!"

"Fine," Danny said, grabbing Josh's arm. "We'll go now."

He and Josh left Petty shouting at the broken picture frame and let themselves out. The door at the foot of the stairs had a deadlock that they could open from the inside, so they got back out into the lobby and then left it to fall shut behind them. The only way back in would be if Petty opened it—or if they S.W.I.T.C.H.ed again.

"Watch from behind our curtains at all times!" scoffed Danny. "What does she think we are— spies? Doesn't she know we have to go to school? And bed?"

"She's going a bit crazy," Josh said. He rubbed his nose and looked worried. "I thought she might if we told her about the marbles."

"Hey—she's lost her marbles!" quipped Danny, but Josh gave him a stony look. "OK, I'll shut up," Danny sighed.

They stepped out into Princessland, trying to act normal again. Or more normal than last time. And then a series of things happened very fast.

First, Josh was knocked over as somebody ran past him. Then someone else tripped over him, cursing loudly, and then a large coat was shoved in his face and then a loud alarm went off.

Danny, who'd gone ahead, trying to avoid looking at the fairy outfits, was spun around by the impact of someone bashing into his shoulder. It was the woman in the long coat, running past him. Her daughter, who wasn't wearing a long coat anymore, was pulling stuff out of her jumper and chucking it on the floor as she skidded after her mother, bawling "Maa! Maaa! Wait for meeeee!"

Danny ran over to Josh, who was struggling out from under the coat. Just as his surprised face emerged there was a shout. "OY! You two! STOP RIGHT THERE!" And a heavy hand landed on Danny's shoulder.

"SO! You think nicking stuff from Princessland is a joke, do you?" said the voice. Danny looked up, shocked, into the face of a burly security guard. "Well, sunshine, I'm calling the police . . . and you two . . ." The guard dragged Josh up by his collar, ". . . are coming with ME!"

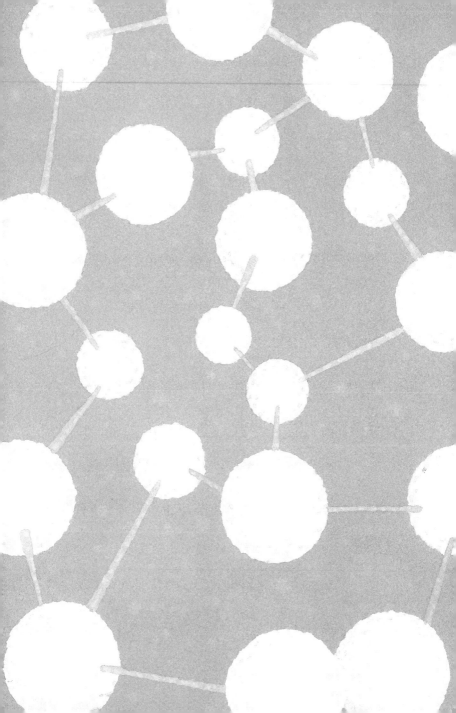

Desperate Diddlies

Josh and Danny were dragged along by their elbows through the shop, loudly protesting their innocence. The store manager, a thin, nervous-looking man in a pale pink shirt, hurried behind them carrying the dumped coat and all the things that had dropped out of it. They all arrived in a small square office with two-way mirror windows, a desk, and three chairs. On the wall was a sign that read "WE ALWAYS PROSECUTE SHOPLIFTERS!" The guard shoved them across the room and pulled the door shut, while the manager hit a button on the wall that silenced the alarm.

"Right!" snapped the security guard. He wore a gray uniform, a peaked cap, and a menacing look on his rather square face. "So . . . let's see what we have here, shall we?" He took the coat and the things bundled up with it and began slapping them all, one by one, onto the desk. "ONE—Diddly DeeDee double doll set. TWO— Diddly DeeDee fashion boots set. THREE—Diddly DeeDee doggy kennel including Diddly Doggy and DiddlyDoggy Dinner Dish."

Danny let out a snort of laughter. He just couldn't help it. The security guard's large sausage-thick fingers paused just as they were about to pluck yet another Diddly DeeDee treat from the coat. "You think this is funny, do you, boy? You thinking cheating us out of Diddly DeeDees is just a joke, do you?"

Danny snorted again. Josh bit his lip. Then they both burst out laughing.

"Have it your way!" snarled the security guard, emptying another ten or twelve packets of Princessland goodies all over the desk, including three yellow toy microphones. "Let's see what the police have to say about this, shall we? Mr. Butch—please call the police!"

"Erm—I'll have to call from the manager's office," Mr. Butch said. "You'd better come with me to verify what's happened . . ."

"Fine—we'll lock these two young thieves in here until they arrive!" the security guard said. And then he and the manager went out and slammed the door shut, locking it firmly behind them.

"Oh dear," gurgled Danny, wiping away tears.

Josh got control. "This is not good, Danny! This is really not good. What will Mom and Dad say when we get arrested? For shoplifting?!"

"We're innocent!" repeated Danny. "They'll believe us! And there must be security cameras or something, where we can show them the real shoplifters!"

"But . . . Mom and Dad will want to know why we were here," pointed out Josh.

Danny's face went serious. "Oh no . . ." he moaned. "What if people we know find out that we were in Princessland? We'll have to move! Leave town!"

"There's only one thing for it," Josh said. "We've got to escape before they make us tell them our names and addresses." He pulled the bottle of GeckoSWITCH out of his pocket. "And this is how!"

Danny jumped to his feet. "Spray me! NOW!"

When the security guard and Mr. Butch came back to tell the two young criminals that the police were on their way, they were shocked into silence. As soon as they unlocked the door and stepped into the tiny office they could see the inmates had vanished. Completely.

"Whaaa-aaa-aaa?" inquired the security guard. Mr. Butch just stood with his mouth opening and closing, no sound coming out. They checked under the desk. In a cupboard. Even behind some coats that hung from hooks on the wall.

"But—but—but . . . how?" spluttered the security guard. His eyes bulged with disbelief. "We locked them in! And that's a proper deadlock, that is! And there's no window to the outside . . . and no way they could have gone through the floor . . . it's solid concrete!"

"Well, I'm . . . flabbergasted!" Mr. Butch said.

They continued to stare all around the room. Eventually they even looked up at the ceiling. If they'd done that as soon as they'd walked in, they might have gotten a clue as to how Danny and Josh escaped. They might have seen a sleek leopard-skinned gecko and a shiny pink gecko dart across the ceiling tiles.

But by the time they'd even thought to look up, Josh and Danny had long since run down the wall and out through the top corner of the open door.

"Who-hoooo! Score!" cheered Danny. They ran speedily along the ceiling of the store, skittering with great ease around light fixtures and suspended signs. It was a fabulous ceiling to walk on—smooth and white with enough obstacles to be fun. He didn't even mind that he was still pink and Josh had got to be the cool leopard-skinned version again.

"Head for the door," called Josh. "We'd better get outside before we change back. We don't want to drop from this height when we S.W.I.T.C.H. back into boyaaaaaaaaaagh!"

At this point, Josh S.W.I.T.C.H.ed back. Two seconds later, Danny did the same.

They both plummeted to the floor.

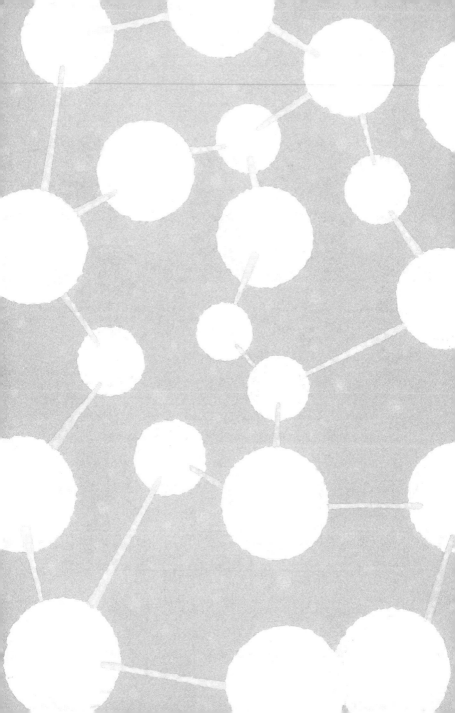

Here Be Dragons

The ceiling was high. A good three meters higher than in a normal house. And beneath it lay sparkly white tiles laid over a solid concrete floor. Had Josh and Danny been a meter off to one side, they would have smacked onto the unforgiving tiles and broken several bones.

Happily, they had been scurrying across the ceiling just above the FLUMPYWUMPY display. A round, shallow, plastic container rather like a large wading pool stood up on six sturdy legs at table height. It was filled with hundreds of Flumpywumpies . . . strange fluff-filled, glittery creatures that were all the rage among girls at school right now. If you pulled a string on a Flumpywumpy's back, it would gurgle, "Flumpywumpy wuvvs you!"

Danny and Josh hit the Flumpywumpies at great velocity, sending a shower of them into the air and over the edge of the display. Several of them told Josh and Danny they "wuvved" them—in spite of the crushing and the throwing.

"Quick!" Josh hissed, scrambling through a multicolored cascade of Flumpwumpies and onto the floor. But as soon as he spoke, he knew something was wrong. His voice was all high and chirrupy—and his vision was astoundingly good. He could see all the detail of the My Tiny Horseys, half an aisle away. "Uh-oh!" he said, turning around to look at Danny. Danny was brushing several Flumpywumpies off his jeans and kicking more back under the display. Right up to his waist, he was back to normal. But above his waist he was still a gecko. Boy sized, but with gecko arms, hands, and fingers. He had a gecko chest and a gecko head covered in gleaming scales of shiny pink, with two dark, bulbous, orblike eyes.

Danny turned and saw Josh a second later. "Oops," he squeaked. He glanced into a mirror in the nearby Barbie display and then over to Josh

again, feeling panic rise in his chest. "We've got to get out of here!"

There was a lot of noise over by the exit. Far, far too many people were around. Loads of little girls in sparkly dresses and tiaras were piling through the doors. Oh no, remembered Danny. The Damsels' Party! But worse, off to their left, Danny could now see the security guard stalking along the top row of toy aisles. They were looking left and right, obviously searching for him and Danny. He might just recognize their jeans and running shoes! "We're just going to have to make a run for it!" he squawked at his brother. And the pair of them set off, making for the doors.

They expected screaming. A lot of it. Danny was hoping the fear and horror would mean the girls would just run away as they approached, clearing their path to the outside world. And true—there was a lot of squealing as they ran up to the doorway. But not the kind they expected. There were about fifteen or sixteen girls and half a dozen moms with them, along with a Princessland entertainer, dressed as a court jester, waving a stick with bells and being determinedly jolly. And as soon as the girls and their moms saw Josh and Danny, both still half-boy, half-gecko, they squealed . . . with DELIGHT!

"Dragons! Oh look! They've got us DRAGONS!" squealed the damsels. And they fell upon Josh and Danny as if they were a basket of free Diddly DeeDees, giggling and cooing and stroking their heads.

"Amazing costumes!" one of the moms said. "So lifelike!"

Josh and Danny were appalled. They were surrounded by a crowd of damsels who were now pulling at their arms and dragging them across to the party area. This was a space right in the middle of Princessland, with lots of little glittery chairs laid out in a circle. Inside the circle was an assortment of girly fun—a large dolls' house, a small fabric tent shaped like a pink castle, dozens of My Tiny Horseys pulling along pumpkin-shaped coaches with princess dolls in them, a hair-braiding table, a bracelet-making corner, and a face-painting stand . . . all laid out for a party.

"Wait!" called a shrill voice. "I know what we're going to do!" It was a girl with curly red hair, topped with a silver tiara, wearing a white frock with pink roses stitched all over it.

"Melissa, sweetheart!" cooed her mom, just behind her. "We're going to make bracelets and have face painting and hair braiding."

"NO!" shouted Melissa. "It's MY party and I say we have a dragon FIGHT!"

The rest of the girls whooped with excitement.

"And this is MY dragon!" Melissa threw her arms around Danny. "Because he's PINK! And that's my favorite color! Who's on my PINK dragon side?!"

Several girls shrieked with approval and got behind Melissa, ready to cheer on the pink dragon.

Another girl with long dark hair and a red dress claimed Josh. "OK—I'll have the spotty dragon!" she sang—and the rest of the girls ran to be on her side.

"My team against Lucy's team!" declared Melissa, as the Princessland entertainer and the moms stood by helplessly. "Our dragons will FIGHT TO THE DEATH!"

Josh and Danny stared at her. They were in Princessland, standing in between two crowds of damsels—and the damsels, with their rosebud dresses and tiaras and shiny ballet shoes . . . wanted them to FIGHT TO THE DEATH?! Danny felt a grudging admiration rise through him. These girls weren't all bad, he decided.

"Darling . . . that seems a bit . . . violent," simpered Melissa's mother.

"Yes, it DOES, doesn't it?" Melissa picked up a long baton from a nearby majorettes twirling sticks display. "Here you are, *Pink* Dragon! Go beat up the spotty dragon!"

A high-pitched roar of approval went up, drowning out the Princessland entertainer's protest. Then the dark-haired girl seized another twirling baton and handed it to Josh. "Bash his brains in, Spotty Dragon!" she urged. The batons were long, silvery sticks with heavy, sparkly balls on either end. As Josh and Danny took one each, they realized these could actually do quite a bit of damage.

"We've got to get out of here!" hissed Josh, glancing all around for an escape route. But they were surrounded by girls—many of them linking arms as they stood whooping and cheering.

"FIGHT! FIGHT! FIGHT! FIGHT!" goaded Melissa.

"Ah come on," grinned Danny, gripping his baton and holding it out between both reptilian fists. "We might as well give them a show . . ."

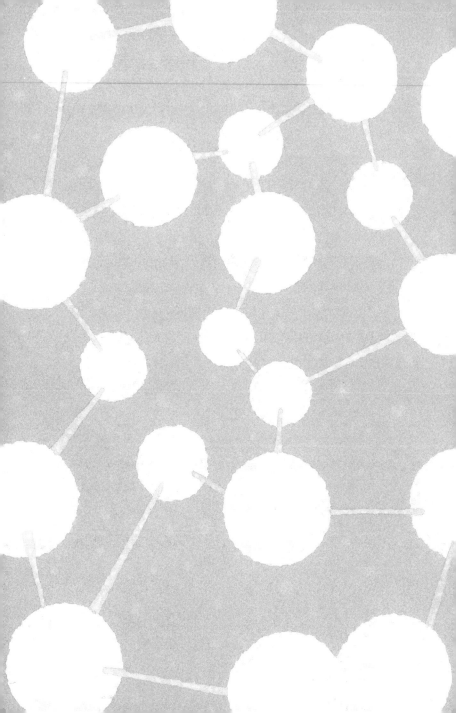

To the Death!

"TO THE DEATH!!!" Danny shrieked as he ran at Josh, holding the baton like a mace. It came out a bit high-pitched and chirrupy.

Josh sighed and sidestepped his brother at the last second. But Danny was expecting that, and he swooped his baton to the left, whacking Josh in the middle of his scaly chest. There was a roar of approval from Melissa's team.

"Gah! Right! You ASKED for it!" squeaked Josh, spinning around and bringing his own baton up to whack Danny on the arm. Lucy's team gave a shrill cry of approval and started chanting "FIGHT! FIGHT! FIGHT! FIGHT!"

Danny let off an angry chirp as the heavy, rounded end of Josh's baton connected with his elbow—and he swung his baton around and thwacked his brother on the ribs.

Then Josh got really angry and bit him. Hard. On the shoulder.

"Yeeeow!" screeched Danny. "That's dirty fighting!"

"Oh yeah?!" grinned Josh, leaping from left to right as his brother tried to land another baton thump on him. "So, what are you going to do about it, Pinkie?!"

Danny let out a cry of rage and threw himself on Josh, snapping his sharp teeth down hard on the back of Josh's neck. Around them, the damsels were in a frenzy of cheering and chanting. And the moms were now trying to shout them down. The Princessland entertainer was waving his little jester's stick around and calling for calm.

Josh shook Danny off and then jumped onto his brother's chest. He snapped his own sharp teeth on Danny's shoulder. A moment later, they were rolling across the party circle floor, knocking over the friendship bracelets stand and sending an avalanche of beads across the tiles.

Josh and Danny were having the times of their lives. They had never fought like this before. They'd scrapped often enough, of course—they were brothers. But a really full-on FIGHT like this? Never!

If Josh hadn't spotted the security guard and the store manager running toward the cacophony, things might have gotten more serious. But seeing Mr. Butch and the square-faced guard helped him remember who he was. And who Danny was and what they had been trying to do when they got caught up in the Damsels' Party. ESCAPE! That's what!

Josh rolled into the pink castle-shaped tent, dragging Danny with him. He hoped desperately that he wasn't about to make things even worse. Out of sight of the baying damsels, he pulled the S.W.I.T.C.H. spray out of his pocket for the third time. He squirted a bit at Danny and then at himself.

Outside, the security guard was already pushing through all the screaming damsels and making for the doorway to the pink tent castle. He looked furious. He'd had more strife in one afternoon in Princessland than he'd ever had working with juvenile delinquents . . .

But then he slid on a slick of friendship bracelet beads and shot across the floor. He shot into the face-paint stand. A large pot landed on his nose, daubing him with glittery yellow. All the damsels burst into fits of uncontrollable giggling.

He struggled onto his knees and crawled toward the tent, growling with fury. But when he tore open the curtains at the tent doorway, he was once again confronted with nothing. Nobody there at all!

"What is GOING ON?!!" he wailed, sinking back down to the floor. "I've been working too hard," he told himself as his forehead thumped onto the floor. An orange flumpywumpy slid down his face. "I wuvv you!" it told him. He didn't notice the leopard-skin and pink geckos shimmying up over his shoulder and shooting out of the castle tent window.

There was a pillar near the pink castle. In fact, the structure had been tied up against it for extra stability. Danny and Josh shot up the pillar so fast that they were nothing more than a blur to anyone watching—and nobody was watching. They were far too interested in seeing whether the big security guard was going to stop crying and come back out of the pink castle.

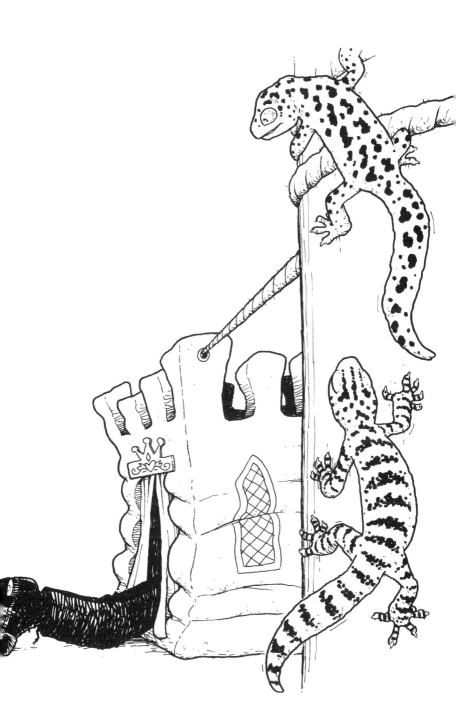

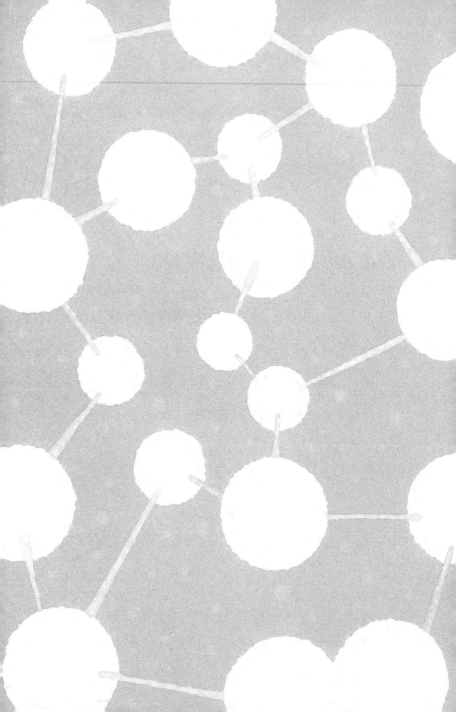

In the Bag

Danny and Josh got outside the store in less than a minute and then shot into some shrubs that grew alongside it. They sat, motionless, waiting to S.W.I.T.C.H. back again. For several minutes, they said nothing. Danny licked his eyeballs once or twice. But other than that, they just kept still.

Finally, Danny spoke. "That was . . . kind of weird." The scales on his shoulder were sore and bruised, even though he'd S.W.I.T.C.H.ed back down to gecko size. The back of Josh's neck was also covered in teeth marks. "Sorry, Josh. I really didn't mean to bite you that hard."

"Yes, you did," Josh said. "But so did I. Don't feel too bad—we couldn't help it."

"What do you mean?" Danny asked. He was feeling very guilty about the great glee with which he had attacked his twin just ten minutes ago.

"We're both geckos, and we're both male," explained Josh. "Female geckos can get along fine together. But male geckos can't. They're really territorial. And they quite often fight to the death."

Danny gulped.

"It's just as well that security guard came along," Josh said. "I might've bitten your head off."

Danny smirked. "I'd like to see you try . . ."

"DON'T!" Josh waved his gecko hand at Danny. "Seriously! DON'T! We mustn't let that happen again. How will I explain it to Mom? She'll ask where are you, and I'll have to say I bit your head off. She won't like it, you know."

"She'll be fine—because I will have bitten YOUR head off!" snarled Danny, getting up onto all four feet and baring his teeth.

FFFFFFFFOOOFFF!

And then he was crouched on his hands and knees with his head poking up out of the bushes, still baring his teeth. Josh was doing the same. Fortunately, they were both boy-shaped again. Completely, this time.

"Phew!" sighed Josh. "That was close. Come on—let's go home. I've had enough excitement for one day."

Danny nodded, getting to his feet and looking around, embarrassed.

They dusted themselves off, noticing that there was still bits of blood on their boy skin and some little bite marks. Then they set out for home.

"WAIT!"

They froze, getting ready to run. Someone was skipping out of Princessland after them.

"WAIT!"

It was Melissa, waving two party bags. "The lady in Princessland said you two were our dragons!" she puffed, as she reached them. "You were so COOL! She said you must have these spare party bags. Here you go! Thanks for the fight!"

And then she was gone, leaving them with the bags.

Danny and Josh turned and ran.

When they got home, they sank gratefully onto the grass in their front garden. Danny started foraging through his party bag. "Cake!" he announced, pulling out a large golden wedge of spongecake topped with thick, pink icing. Josh found one too, and they both stuffed the cake into their mouths, super hungry after all the excitement.

"What else?" murmured Danny, digging into the bag again. "Bracelet—eurgh!" He chucked a stretchy beaded bracelet onto the grass. "Diddly DeeDee! Oh no! I never want to see another Diddly DeeDee!" He chucked that on top of the bracelet. "Jelly beans! Woohoo! Kazoo . . . not bad. And . . ." Then he stopped, puzzled. At the bottom of the bag was a bit of wadded-up notepaper.

"Jo-osh . . ." he said.

Josh had been going through his bag too, finding all the same things . . . and now . . . he too had some wadded-up paper.

What made them both go very quiet and still

was the familiar spiky writing. They opened up the notes and saw they were exactly the same. Each read:

HELLO AGAIN, JOSH AND DANNY.
AMAZING ESCAPE!
YOU ARE BOTH SO WORTHY
OF THE DESTINY THAT
AWAITS YOU . . .
DARE YOU SEEK IT?

Danny gulped and stared at Josh. "The Mystery Marble Sender!" he whispered. "They must have been right there in Princessland—watching us!"

"I know," breathed Josh, glancing all around them. "They could be here now!" He shivered.

They read the next bit of their notes. The bit that always came next . . . the clue.

DON'T BLOW OR SUCK—HUM IF YOU CAN.
AND IF YOU CAN'T—YOU WIN!

"What?" Danny stared at the note. "What kind of a clue is that?"

But Josh was smiling. "An easy one. Which is just as well, because I'm not doing anything else good. No more adventures! I need a break!"

"You've just turned into your own granny," observed Danny. But he knew what Josh meant. They needed a break from weirdness for a while.

Josh picked up both the kazoos. "Here you go," he said, handing one to Danny. It was a good quality one, chunky and made of metal. "Blow in it, and it won't work. Sucking on it won't work either."

"No! You have to hum!" cried Danny, and he stuck the kazoo in his mouth, closed his lips around it, and hummed a little tune. It came out as a lively buzz.

"You can hum," Josh said. "So you don't win. Now let's see . . ."

He put the other kazoo to his lips and started humming. Nothing came out except a dull murmur. No buzzing. No humming. Josh grinned at Danny. "I win," he said.

And he tugged at the little round porthole-style window on the top of the metal barrel until it came off. Underneath this should have been a piece of tissue paper. But instead, he found something small and round. A lump of glass.

He tipped it onto his palm.

One perfect glass marble with a ribbon of color running through it. Getting out his magnifying glass, Josh could just make out the code inside—and the hologram of what looked like . . . a whale. "Yup—it's another S.W.I.T.C.H. marble," he confirmed. "But I think this one must be for you," he chuckled, handing it to Danny.

"Oh very funny," Danny said.

The marble was pink.

Top Secret!

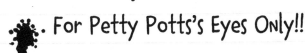

. For Petty Potts's Eyes Only!!

DIARY ENTRY 701.2

SUBJECT: NEW HOME

What a relief to finally have the new laboratory set up! And it was good that Josh and Danny managed to follow my instructions and get in here so easily after S.W.I.T.C.H.ing into geckos. Very handy spray, that! They're much less vulnerable as reptiles than they would be as insects—and they can walk up walls and along ceilings and through cracks. They'd make excellent burglars or spies . . . now that is a thought for the future.

The only problem is the ongoing instability of REPTOSWITCH. I really must get to the bottom of it because it's the second time a lizard S.W.I.T.C.H. has gone a little off-kilter. And of course, the amphibian one was problematic too. And the two species are very closely related. I must find out what's going wrong.

Mind you, Josh and Danny seemed fine today and obviously got home again unscathed and without further incident. I'm probably worrying too much!

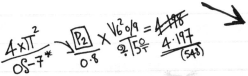

Meanwhile, I must also study the S.W.I.T.C.H. marbles and the notes that came with them to try to discover who this Mystery Marble Sender is. It is most unnerving! Could it be Victor Crouch, alive and well after all this time, trying to mess with my genius mind? But why? If he had stolen my code for MAMMALSWITCH, surely he would just claim it as his own—wouldn't he?

Something about those notes keeps bothering me..."Dare you seek your Destiny?" It says that every time. But why? There is something very familiar about that sentence...I MUST remember! I MUST! I MUST!

I will now go and hit the back of my skull repeatedly with a frying pan. Sometimes that works. Better find a clean one, though. Last time I remembered three things—but had scrambled egg stuck in my hair for a week...

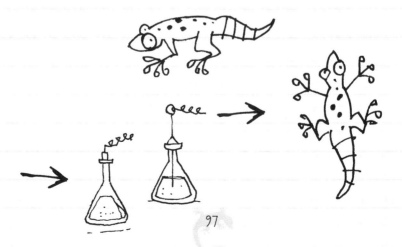

GLOSSARY

amphibian: an animal that can live on land and in water

antidote: something that takes away the bad effects of a poison or disease

arachnid: A member of the group of animals that includes spiders and scorpions

cellular: made from cells

hijack: to take control of something by force

hologram: a type of photograph made by laser beams. A hologram appears to have depth as well as height and width.

laboratory: a room or building equipped for scientific work

mammal: any animal of which the female gives birth to live young and can feed them with her own milk

pigment: a substance that colors something

prosecute: to prosecute someone is to make them go to a court of law to be tried for a crime

reptile: a cold-blooded animal that creeps or crawls. Lizards and snakes are reptiles.

scales: the thin, overlapping parts on the outside of fish, snakes, and other animals

serum: a kind of fluid used in science and for medical purposes

setae: small hairlike pads responsible for the animal's ability to cling to vertical surfaces

snout: the front part sticking out from an animal's head, with its nose and mouth

territorial: an animal that guards and is defensive of an area of land it believes to be its own

transparent: something you can see through

Recommended Reading

BOOKS

Want to brush up on your reptile and amphibian knowledge? Here's a list of books dedicated to slithering and hopping creatures.

Johnson, Jinny. *Animal Planet™ Wild World: An Encyclopedia of Animals*. Minneapolis: Millbrook Press, 2013.

McCarthy, Colin. *Reptile*. DK Eyewitness Books. New York: DK Publishing, 2012.

Parker, Steve. *Pond & River*. DK Eyewitness Books. New York: DK Publishing, 2011.

WEBSITES

Find out more about nature and wildlife using the websites below.

National Geographic Kids

http://kids.nationalgeographic.com/kids/
Go to this website to watch videos and read facts about your favorite reptiles and amphibians.

San Diego Zoo Kids

http://kids.sandiegozoo.org/animals
Curious to learn more about some of the coolest-looking reptiles and amphibians? This website has lots of information and stunning pictures of some of Earth's most interesting creatures.

US Fish & Wildlife Service

http://www.nwf.org/wildlife/wildlife-library
/amphibians-reptiles-and-fish.aspx
Want some tips to help you look for wildlife in your own neighborhood? Learn how to identify some slimy creatures and some scaly ones as well.

CHECK OUT ALL OF THE

Spider Stampede
by Ali Sparkes illustrated by Ross Collins

Ant Attack
by Ali Sparkes illustrated by Ross Collins

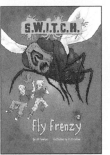

Fly Frenzy
by Ali Sparkes illustrated by Ross Collins

Crane Fly Crash
by Ali Sparkes illustrated by Ross Collins

Grasshopper Glitch
by Ali Sparkes illustrated by Ross Collins

Beetle Blast
by Ali Sparkes illustrated by Ross Collins

 **TITLES!**

Frog Freakout

Newt Nemesis

Lizard Loopy

Chameleon Chaos

Turtle Terror

Gecko Gladiator

Anaconda Adventure

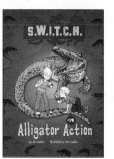
Alligator Action

About the Author

Ali Sparkes grew up in the wilds of the New Forest, raised by sand lizards who taught her the secret language of reptiles and how to lick her own eyes.

At least, that's how Ali remembers it. Her family argues that she grew up in a house in Southampton, raised by her mom and dad, who taught her the not terribly secret language of English and wished she'd stop chewing her hair.

She once caught a slow worm. It flicked around like mad, and she was a bit scared and dropped it.

Ali still lives in Southampton, now with her husband and two sons. She likes to hang out in the nearby wildlife center, spying on common lizards. The lizards are considering legal action . . .

About the Illustrator

Ross Collins's more than eighty picture books and books for young readers have appeared in print around the world. He lives in Scotland and, in his spare time, enjoys leaning backward precariously in his chair.